THIS BOOK BELONGS TO

MY FAVOURITE POEM IS

ALPHABETICAL POETICAL - 1

Steve Morley was born in Bradford in Yorkshire. He had a number of different jobs before becoming a trainee teacher. He reluctantly abandoned teaching training to become a champion chicken slaughterer for which he was given the nickname Claudius, because 'he murdered most foul'. After a short spell in uniform, with Bradford City Transport, he left for the bright lights of London to pursue a career as an actor, a profession that has intermittently entertained him for more than forty years.

For over a decade Steve played Sergeant Lamont in TV's ever popular *The Bill* (for which he also worked as a script writer); this was a part he was eternally grateful for as he appeared so infrequently no-one ever recognised him. But forget the world tours of great Shakespearean roles, forget the trip to Hollywood, forget even fighting Cybermen and being the vet in *Emmerdale*, Steve still regards his greatest claim to fame as winning an award for being the first man to appear nude on Irish radio.

In 2006 Steve was nominated for the national award of Teacher of the Year.

In 2010 *The Nutting Plays* and *The Farmhouse Plays* were nominated for a Company of Educators' Award.

In 2020 Steve retired from teaching at the City of London School for Girls where he had been Director of Drama for twenty years.

ALPHABETICAL POETICAL - 1

by Steve Morley

Humorous verse for kids

ALPHABETICAL POETICAL - 1
© Steve Morley 2021

CONDITION OF SALE

ALL ENQUIRIES

mrsteve.morley@outlook.com

For Thalia and Theo…

…and with thanks to Jo Russell and Jenny Brown

Alphabetical Poetical Theoretical

Alphabetical poetical,
For now it's theoretical
If I can write some poems for each letter.
To go from A to Zed
Might do things to my head,
But maybe by the end I'll be much better…

I'll really have to wait and see
If I can get past letter B,
Perhaps I will get stuck before the C.
But if I do not try
I won't get to letter Y,
Let alone the one Americans call Zee…

So let's give it a try,
Wish me luck, wave me goodbye,
Because if I don't start I'll never know.
I must swallow all my fears
Of this taking thirty years,
Alphabetical Poetical…

…here we go…

Almighty Bamboozle

Don't ever disturb the almighty Bamboozle
Because if you do you will certainly lose-le.
If he wakes up mad, he will give you a bruise-le,
So NEVER disturb the sleeping Bamboozle.

It's said now and then that the mighty Bamboozle
Is not quite all there with a few missing screws-le,
He's mad and he's bad, he sinks ships with their crews-le,
So NEVER disturb the napping Bamboozle.

Do not question why the almighty Bamboozle
Is blocking your way while he's having a snooze-le,
Just thank all the stars that there's just one Bamboozle
And NEVER disturb the snoring Bamboozle.

So don't ever think you might wake the Bamboozle
By playing some music or singing the Blues-le.
He'll bash you and mash you right to Timbuktuzle
So NEVER disturb,
No NEVER disturb,
Don't EVER, not EVER, no matter the weather,
Don't EVER disturb the almighty Bamboozle!

~ ~ ~ ~ ~

This space is left for those who wish to draw the
ALMIGHTY BAMBOOZLE

Anyway...
(The never-ending poem)

I really like the words that rhyme,
I use them all the time.
I really like the taste of lime
But not when dipped in...
...anyway.

An Indian burn upon the arm
Can catch you unaware
And if it's done quite viciously
Can make you want to...
...anyway.

Henry the Eighth loved Anne Boleyn
But not when she was dead.
Because it's hard to love someone
If they don't have a...
...anyway.

Some dogs they like to wee on trees,
It stops them being glum.
Then they meet in the street and say,
"Please, may I sniff your..."
...anyway.

When you've eaten too much grub
You don't know what to do.
You only hope you're not in class
If you need a...
...anyway.

I had a dream the other day,
It really was quite rude.

I stood there on the stage at school
And I was in the…
…anyway.

My friend is jumping up and down,
Right there for all to see,
And we all know she needs to go
Outside to have a…
…anyway.

We were so hot in class today
While waiting for the bell,
But teacher said, "Please go away,
I cannot stand the…"
…anyway.

So don't forget that poetry
Is with us all the time
But it won't always work if you
Do not have a…

~ ~ ~ ~ ~

Asparrowgrass

The sparrow in the grass
Was looking for asparagus,
But little did he know
That many years ago,
The word asparagus
Was back then known as sparrow grass.

~ ~ ~ ~ ~

B's

I really like the letter B,
I like the things it does,
I can't say *why* I like those things,
B's just give me a buzz.

~ ~ ~ ~ ~

Bob The Butcher

My old friend Bob the Butcher,
Is a most special guy,
And once he asked a favour,
To reach something on high.
Two bits of meat were gathered
Up there on a shelf,
And he could not go near them
(It's not good for his health).
But I had to turn him down,
This really special guy,
For when I'd thought about it,
The steaks were far too high.

~ ~ ~ ~ ~

Burp Song

(Readers are invited to create their own music to this song.)

My friend, when going to his job,
Stopped by the local shop,
To buy a great big bottle
Of fizzy, ginger pop.
And when at last he got to work
He took a massive slurp,
Then he went in the crowded lift
Where he began to burp.

The lift was full of office folk,
Who looked with some surprise,
At my old friend who thought it best
To use a neat disguise.
So he looked at the people there
And shouted, 'Sing along!'
And that's when he began to turn
His burps into a song.

CHORUS   *Oh it was wrong*
So very wrong
Turning his burps into a song
Within a lift
Burps in a lift
On oh so many levels it was wrong.

The first song that he burped to them
Made them look all about,
Considering that they might need
To turf this burpist out,
But the song was all about a
Very funny devil,
And well before they'd realised
They'd reached the second level.

CHORUS

The second song that he then burped
Had them all in stitches.
'Twas all about an arsonist
Who set fire to his breeches
The fire brigade they put him out
Making him quite porous
And as the third floor passed them by
They all burped the chorus

CHORUS

By the fourth floor the song he burped
Smelled of pickled herring.
The people there could not believe
What each nose was smelling.
But then he burped a song about
A glue that never sticks,
And well before they knew it, they
Had got to level six

CHORUS   .

The final song he burped to them
Concerned the girl next door,
This girl was rather desperate,
Cos she was very poor.
The song was oh so sad they wept
And never saw him go,
Leaving them all to go back down
Right to the bottom floor.

CHORUS, THEN CHORUS WITH ECHO
Oh it was wrong (Oh it was wrong)
So very wrong   (So very wrong)
Turning his burps into a song   (Into a song)
Within a lift (Within a lift)
Burps in a lift   (Burps in a lift)
(All together)   On oh so many levels it was wrong!

~ ~ ~ ~ ~

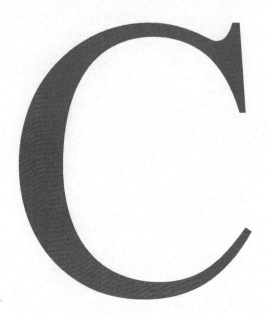

Canoes

Canoes are very difficult,
They're boats made just for you.
Not for anyone else at all,
Certainly not for two.
They're very hard to row at first,
You could turn upside down,
And as they don't have any wheels,
They're very bad in town.
So if you find yourself in one,
I'll tell you what to do,
Canoes don't worry me at all,
'Cos I can row - canoe?

~ ~ ~ ~ ~

Claire

There was a young woman called Claire,
Whose face was all covered with hair.
When she went for a walk
The neighbours would talk,
Saying, "Look, there goes Paddington Bear!"

~ ~ ~ ~ ~

Clerihew

E. Clerihew Bentley
Went on to invent the
Verse form known as the clerihew.
Its fame began there – then it grew.

*The clerihew is a verse form consisting of two rhyming couplets of
unequal length, the first line always being the name of a person.
There is another in this book, see if you can spot it.*

~ ~ ~ ~ ~

Déjà vu

Déjà vu is a feeling that you have already experienced something that is currently happening.

Déjà vu is the name
Of the verse I wish to write.
But I have this strange feeling,
I wrote it the other night.

~ ~ ~ ~ ~

Dingo

I used to know a dingo,
A very quiet dog,
Quite unlike his brother,
Who snored just like a hog.

He was a cleanly dingo,
A neat and tidy dog,
Quite unlike his mother,
Who wallowed in a bog.

He always bought you presents
A very generous dog,
Quite unlike his sister
Whose name was Selfish Mog.

He always did the washing up,
A very helpful dog,
Quite unlike his father,
As lazy as a frog.

I asked my friend the dingo,
This very quiet dog,
What made him be so peaceful,
As silent as the fog?

And do you know what he said...?

He said:
'Did you know that from a very early age
I desperately wanted to be a Hush Puppy,
and so, one day,
I just thought and thought and thought and
thought and thought and thought out loud so all
could hear me, until my brains were nearly raw
with all the effort and I was getting a terrible
pain in my tummy, and everybody was nearly
deaf with listening to me, until, at last…
…I just closed my mouth...
            ...and made the din go.'

~ ~ ~ ~ ~

Diddle-Hey-**D**iddle

Diddle-hey-diddle,
The cat played her fiddle,
The spoon ran away with the dish.
"Oh, cow," said the moon,
"Jump over me soon,
And I'll grant your every wish."

So the cow took a run
From the spot she'd begun,
And she leapt right over the moon,
She came down as a steak
For the small boy to bake,
And to eat with the help of the spoon.

Then the boy made the wish,
As he finished his dish,
And he asked for a very long time,
Which would pass so that he
Never ever would be
In such a mixed-up nursery rhyme.

~ ~ ~ ~ ~

What nursery rhyme is this poem based on?

Earwigs

Earwigs are so stupid,
A silly matching pair.
They stop your earwax getting out,
But cover your ears with hair.
Earwigs bamboozle me,
I cannot make them out.
If they're worn in conversation,
The people have to shout.

Earwigs astonish me,
They really are a riddle.
How can you ever hope to part
An earwig down the middle?
Earwigs are confusing,
Their prospects are quite grim,
How can you ever see to know,
If one's needing a trim.

Earwigs bedazzle me,
They really hurt my head.
Wouldn't it be more sensible,
To wear a nosewig instead?
Nosewigs do enthral me,
They put me at my ease.
They'd stop the germs from spreading,
After a great big sneeze.

Nosewigs do amuse me,
A wig upon your conk!
And nobody will ever know

It was you who gave that honk!
But earwigs are useless,
Like rubber garden shears.
So why do we need wigs at all,
Especially on our ears?

P.S. There is a song about a particular earwig who was
called Oh.
You may remember it. It goes like this:

Earwig Oh, Earwig Oh, Earwig Oh,
Earwig Oh, Earwig Oh, Earwig O-Oh,
Earwig Oh, Earwig Oh, Earwig Oh,
Earwig O-Oh, Earwig Oh...
And so on...

~ ~ ~ ~ ~

Eating Caterpillars

I have recently been eating
Quite a lot of caterpillars,
All because those caterpillars are quite yummy.
I would like to tell the whole world
Of my taste for caterpillars,
But sadly, I have butterflies in my tummy.

~ ~ ~ ~ ~

Echo

I say *I say*

I say

Stop repeating what I say,

stop it *stop it*

stop it

I want you to stop it.

and then *and then*

and then

I'm going to count to ten and then

cop it *cop it*

cop it

You're really going to cop it…

one *one*

One…

two *two*

Two…

three *three*

Three…

four *four*

Four…

five *fiEe*

Five…

six *six*

Six…

seven *seven*

Seven…

…eight…

Eight…

…nine…

Nine…

Okay!

T…

~ ~ ~ ~ ~

A Funny Girl Is Mary

Mary had a little lamb,
    It grew up quite contrary,
        But when it ate the other lambs,
            Everyone blamed Mary.

Mary had a little goose,
    Feathered not, but hairy,
        But when it went and kicked the horse,
            All around blamed Mary.

Mary had a little goat,
    Dressed just like a fairy,
        But when it vanished with a flash,
            All the town blamed Mary.

Mary had a little gun,
    She blasted all the prairie,
        And when she threatened all the town,
            No-one dared blamed Mary.

Mary's now a little lamb,
    Not at all contrary,
        But everyone around agrees,
            A funny girl is Mary.

~ ~ ~ ~ ~

♭ Flatfish ♭

Flatfish hit with a rolling pin,
Flatfish battered with a bat,
Flatfish can't sing sharp as a pin,
No wonder this fish is flat.

~ ~ ~ ~ ~

First Day At School

The first day that I went to school,
I didn't know a single rule
The other kids just had to tell me all.
"There is one person here," they'd say,
"You must look up to every day,
You'll meet him when we all go to the hall.

You'll know this person straight away,
And you must never disobey
Or you'll have nightmares when you go to bed.
He isn't big, he isn't small,
But you'll shiver if he should call,
He is the person who we all here dread!"

I stood before them, full of fear,
They took me to a door quite near,
"This dreadful monster lives in there," they said.
"He has no body, has no limbs,
He rests upon a chair and grins."
And then they told me that his name was…

….Head.

~ ~ ~ ~ ~

Galileo

Galileo made a telescope
To see the universe,
And what he saw when looking through
Put thinking in reverse.
Back in those days it was believed
The sun moved round the earth,
You could not think the other way
For all that you were worth.
But Galileo called it out,
The bosses called him in
And said that they would take his life,
He had committed sin.
He tried to argue his ideas,
But was broken-hearted,
And so the sun and earth both went
Back to where they started.

~ ~ ~ ~ ~

Girl With A Lithp

There wath a young girl with a lithp,
Who looked like a will of the withp,
When she floated higher,
She caught all on fire,
And tho she wath thinged to a crithp.

~ ~ ~ ~ ~

Grandad's Snowball Spiders

"There's spiders inside us," my grandad once said,
"They eat our insides up, until we are dead."
"But how did they get there?" I wanted to know.
He answered, "They get there by hiding in snow.

When you make up snowballs and throw them around,
You pick all the snow up from off of the ground.
You have no idea what's hiding inside,
But spiders are clever and in snow they hide.

Then if a big snowball hits you with great pace,
The spiders shoots in through the holes in your face.
It crawls through your body like some sneaky mouse,
And into your stomach, where it sets up house.

And there it will eat you throughout every day,
Until you are so thin there's nothing to weigh."
My grandad, he told this, when I was a kid,
And from that day forward I watched what I did.

I never went outside with snowballs to fight,
I'd have to stay indoors, shaking with fright.
And so I stayed like this for many a year,
Frightened of spiders coming in through my ear.

Now I am grown up I see what was done,
My grandad was teasing, was just having fun.
But I am determined to get my own back,
(If he weren't an old man, I'd give him a smack).

I put snow in his tea, put snow in his shoes,
He picks up his paper, there's snow in the news.
And when to the toilet he finds he must go,
He sits and he finds it's all filled up with snow.

And as for the moral, I will now confide,
Don't scare kids with spiders eating their insides.
Revenge might well take years, but it's sure to come,
When you're on the toilet and freeze off your bum!

~ ~ ~ ~ ~

Hero Me

I'd like to be a pop singer,
A hero in the charts.
I'd sing and croon and make girls swoon
And break a thousand hearts.

I'd like to be a footballer,
A hero on the pitch.
From pole to pole I'd score great goals
And end up filthy rich.

I'd like to be a film actor,
A hero on the set.
I would go far, the greatest star,
An Oscar I will get.

I'd like to be an astronaut,
A hero out in space,
I'd blast to bits those alien ships
And save the human race.

I'd like to be a scientist,
A hero in the lab,
I'd find the cures for plagues and sores,
A Nobel prize I'll grab.

I'd like to be a president,
A hero of world peace.
I would not pause to stop all wars
And make the fighting cease.

I'd like to be an activist,
A hero they'll not beat.
I'd save the trees then clean the seas,
And cool the planet's heat.

My mum says I'm the perfect kid,
A hero to a T,
She says no-one comes near her son,
And that's enough for me!

~ ~ ~ ~ ~

Humpty Dumpty

Humpty Dumpty sat in a tree,
Humpty Dumpty needed a wee.
All the king's horses said to the king's men,
Put up your umbrellas it's raining again.

~ ~ ~ ~ ~

Hunger

There's lumps in the custard,
There's warts on the meat,
There's fire in the mustard,
There's nothing to eat.

There's string in spaghetti,
There's fur on the jam,
I'm not being petty,
I'm starving, I am!

There's bugs in the jelly,
There's mould on the cheese,
My poor aching belly,
I'm down on my knees.

There's dust in the corn flakes,
There's muck in the tea,
The eyes in the spuds
Are staring at me.

The bread's gone all mouldy,
The scones have run out,
Not one Garibaldi,
What's it all about?

The cakes have no Jaffa,
The tarts have no jam,
Can't find me a cracker
And no trace of ham.

No puff in the pastry,
No choc with the ice,
There's nothing that's tasty,
Nothing that's nice.

No rice with the pudding,
No fruit with the pie,
No sage with the stuffing,
I think I might die.

My sandwich is empty,
I haven't a sweet,
I've nothing to tempt me,
I've nothing to eat.

But what's this? A sparrow?
Twittering heaven!
Where's my bow and arrow?
I'm dining at seven!

~ ~ ~ ~ ~

32

I'd Rather Like To Stick Around

The world is a story
We all play our part,
And we all know its history
Right from the start,
But I will miss this world
And all of its trends,
'Cos I'd rather like to stick around
Just to see how it ends

~ ~ ~ ~ ~

I Cannot Get Up In The Morning

The bed is so warm,
And I'm safe from harm,
Outside a new day is dawning.
It's out of my view,
Whatever I do,
I cannot get up in the morning.

I'm still half asleep,
And dreaming of deep
Beautiful things, oh so warming.
I don't have to prove
I'm able to move.
I cannot get up in the morning.

I'm one sleepy head,
Curled up in my bed,
Don't care about winds outside storming,
It's cosy in here,
With nothing to fear,
I cannot get up in the morning.

I don't, as a rule,
       Not once dream of school
              Subjects that I am on form in.
                    It's better to dream,
                        Of chocolate ice cream,
                              I cannot get up in the morning.
Dreaming of such things,
       Alarm clock, it rings,
              It always explodes without warning.
                    I throw it aside,
                        'Neath duvet I'll hide.
                              I cannot get up in the morning.
I go back to sleep,
       Like Little Bo Peep,
              Counting the sheep that are forming.
                    I'll lie here all day,
                      Much nicer this way,
                              I cannot get up in the morning.
It's warm and it's snug,
       Soft pillow to hug,
              The rest of the world I'm ignoring
                    I'm one sleepy head,
                    I do love my bed,
                              I cannot get up in the morning.

~ ~ ~ ~ ~

Island Wish

I'd like to be an island
Off the coast of Italy
My Grandad says, "That's all very well,
But don't you be Sicily"!

~ ~ ~ ~ ~

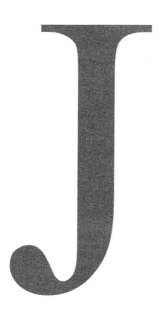

Just Love Sweets!

I just love sweets!
They're really mega treats,
I like them so much better than roast beef.
Given my way
I'd eat them every day,
Making sure I always brush my teeth.

You can not beat,
A chocky or a sweet,
To chomp upon when watching your TV.
I do confess,
They really are the best.
And I'll munch sweets for all eternity!

~ ~ ~ ~ ~

Jazzy

Jazzy was a lovely kid
Who said that she loved verse,
But people said she must be mad
And sent her to the nurse.

The nurse took a good look at her,
She really took her time,
Then gave her a prescription
All written out in rhyme.

She took it to a chemist
(Confused inside her head),
The chemist read it all out loud,
And this is what it said:

"Give this kid a paint brush,
Some paint to stand the weather,
Then send her to a wall to write:
'POETRY FOREVER!'"

~ ~ ~ ~ ~

Jonathan Jilt

Jonathan Jilt hung from a kilt,
And swung from a sporran too,
The Scotsman in question
Had bad indigestion
So now he lives in the loo.

Christopher Katt murdered a rat,
And jumped on a fish as well,
Because of the slaughter
Of his only daughter
He lives in a prison cell.

Barnaby Budge ate all the fudge,
He ate all the curds and whey,
The swell in his belly
Began to get smelly
And so they took him away.

Christabelle Cake jumped in a lake,
And leapt off a bridge so high,
Because of her landings
And misunderstandings,
She's constantly in the sky.

Jonathan Jilt and Mister Katt,
Met Barnaby Budge and Cake,
And now willy-nilly,
They do things so silly,
They keep everyone awake.

~ ~ ~ ~ ~

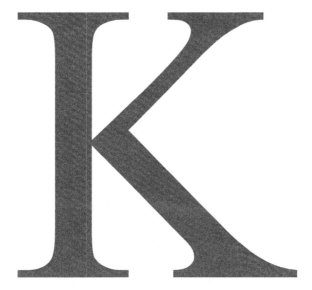

Kakapo and Kiwi

The kakapo and kiwi birds
Went out one day for tea
Deciding then between themselves
To fly above the sea
But though they thought they'd planned it all
The future wasn't bright
For kakapo and kiwi birds
Are neither blessed with flight

~ ~ ~ ~ ~

Kelly

There was an old lady called Kelly,
Who became quite well known on the telly.
It wasn't the fact
She could sing or could act,
But because she was awfully smelly.

~ ~ ~ ~ ~

Kollide-a-Scope

My father bought a telescope,
To see the Moon and Mars,
He swung it round, it hit his head,
And now he's seeing stars.

He staggered all about the room,
I asked him what he saw,
"Colliding with this scope," he said,
"I think has broke my jaw."

"I thought I'd bought a telescope,"
He said, and held his head,
"But now I see that I have a
Kollide-a-Scope instead."

~ ~ ~ ~ ~

Larry Dann

Mummy Dann, said to her young man,
I think I'll call you Garry.
But Larry Dann said to his Mam,
"I'm perfectly happy as Larry."

*'Happy as Larry' is a common expression originating in
Australia and thought to derive from the word 'larrikin', an
Australian term for an unruly young man.*

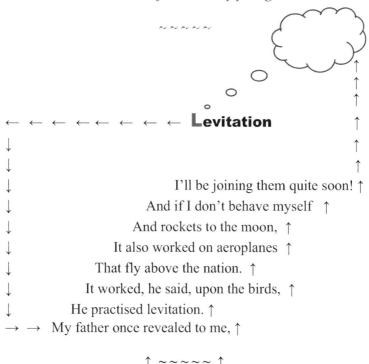

← ← ← ← ← ← ← ← **L**evitation

I'll be joining them quite soon! ↑
And if I don't behave myself ↑
And rockets to the moon, ↑
It also worked on aeroplanes ↑
That fly above the nation. ↑
It worked, he said, upon the birds, ↑
He practised levitation. ↑
→ → My father once revealed to me, ↑

↑ ~ ~ ~ ~ ~ ↑

Lucky

My friend Lucky has lost his leg,
He hops the streets and he tries to beg,
There's just one thing he hopes to do,
Find someone to buy his other shoe

My friend Lucky has lost his eye,
He only sees half the things pass by,
There's just one thing he hopes will pass,
Find some glasses with only one glass.

My friend Lucky has lost his arm,
Why he should, he never did no harm,
There's just one thing he wants for sure,
Find a man to teach him semaphore.

My friend Lucky has lost his nose,
Where it moved to nobody knows,
There's just one thing he wants like hell,
To find some flowers that he can smell.

My friend Lucky has lost his mind,
He hops the streets and he tries to find,
Leg, arm and nose and someone kind
To show him the man who made him blind.

How unkind for one so plucky,
To be saddled with a name...
                    ...the likes of...
                              ...Lucky.

~ ~ ~ ~ ~

My Brother Swallowed a Torch!

My brother swallowed a torch!
I had hidden it in his drink.
Such a silly thing to do,
Ridiculous, you must think.
I just stood and stared at him
As he drank and emptied the cup,
But it was really worth it
When the whole of his face lit up!

~ ~ ~ ~ ~

Max Morley

Max Morley once said to his Mummy,
"I'd love to blow air on your tummy!"
So he blew and he blew.
Till the raspberries grew,
Saying, "Mummy, your tummy is yummy!"

~ ~ ~ ~ ~

Maths

Learn your lessons if you've any sense,
    Like your English and also your French.
        Learn them all (like swimming in the baths),
            But most of all you must learn your maths.

Maths is useful, maths is really fun,
    Maths helps you do what needs to be done.
        Maths will stop you going truly mad,
            Maths will also show you how to add.

Maths will prevent you from getting sacked,
    By showing the boss you can subtract.
        Think of the things that you can now do,
            Like counting animals in the zoo.

Maths will feed you any time of day,
    Come let me show you my take-away.
        Counting the chips needed for the fry?
            Got some more people? Then multiply.

Maths will help you know how many times,
    Twos go into six and threes into nines.
        Maths will help you count all the toads,
            That run from the river down the roads.

Maths lets you count the legs of the bees,
    It's really cool cos it's the bees' knees!
        Maths will show you (it's easily done),
            How to count the bubbles in your gum.

Maths will say (it comes as no surprise),
    What will happen with your multiplies,
        Two times three equals eight less two,
BUT IF YOU HAVEN'T GOT A CALCULATOR..
            ...GOD BLESS YOU!

~ ~ ~ ~ ~

Noose

Any old goose can tell that a noose
Is made for things to hang in.
And any old snake can see at a shake,
It's not for placing fangs in.

Any old horse can see, why of course,
A noose is not for facing.
And any old goat can see that its throat
Is not a thing to place in.

Any old moose will say that a noose,
Is not a thing for fetching.
And any old goose will say that a noose,
Was what its neck got stretched in.

~ ~ ~ ~ ~

Nose

I looked at you…

       …as you picked your nose

I watched you…

       …where you sat

And I realised…

       …if I'd picked your nose

I'd have picked one…

       …better than that

~ ~ ~ ~ ~

Not Last Night

Not last night but the night before,
A Grizzly knocked upon my door.
"Please sir, please sir," he growled at me,
"A dog sir, dog sir, did you see?"
"No sir, no sir," I said to he,
"Not by the skins of my old tee-pee."

Not last night but the night before,
A dog did knock upon my door.
"Woof, sir, woof sir," he barked and spat,
"But have you seen a bad Tom Cat?"
"No sir, no sir, and I must stress,
Not by the feathers on my headdress."

Not last night but one before that,
Door did knock and there stood a cat.
"Please sir, please sir," he hissed at me,
"Was a mouse looking out for me?"
"No cat, no cat," I said to Tom,
"Not by the bangs on my old war drum."

Not last night but two nights ago,
Came there a knocking soft and slow,
A mouse stood there and squeaked to me,
"Please can I hide in your tee-pee?"

"Yes mouse, yes mouse," I said, "of course,
"Hide behind the ears of my best horse."

Not tonight but the night before,
Knocks were loud upon my door.
There stood Grizzly, Dog and Cat,
Come to find where the mouse was at
"Here sirs, here," I said with a bow,
Then we began on a long pow-wow.

Not last night, nor the night before,
Tonight it is and on the floor,
Grizzly, Dog and Cat and Mouse,
Drink the health of all in the house.
Smiles all round, hostilities cease,
As they sit and smoke the pipe of peace.

~ ~ ~ ~ ~

Owl

The big old owl just said to me,
"Do you have any sweets?
I like it when you give me some,
I love those little treats."
I said that I was sorry that
There were no sweets today,
"Regretfully," I said to him,
"I gave them all away."
The owl, he simply looked at me,
And with no more to-do,
He narrowed his big eyes and said,
"You twit. To who? To who?"

~ ~ ~ ~ ~

Online Bird

Have you ever had a word with an online bird
Who never ever wants to meet,
For if you have a word with this online bird
You'll see he just prefers to tweet!

~ ~ ~ ~ ~

Oak Tree Making

A common deciduous forest tree,
Is the gnarled old oak,
And if your interest is forestry,
You'll be glad I spoke.

To make a deciduous forest tree,
As the said old oak,
You run along to an acorn tree
And with a stick – poke

Until an ingenuous acorn drops
Down upon the ground,
Making quite sure that the acorn stops
From rolling round.

Now take this ridiculous egg-like thing,
Sitting in its shell,
Give it a shake like a bell you ring
And with your nose - smell.

The smell is deliciously acorn-like,
Nutty in its way,
Reminding you of the things you like,
Pleasant, I should say.

Now with no maliciously hostile thoughts,
Plant it - add some rain,
And leave it alone for twenty years...
                                    ...then begin again.

~ ~ ~ ~ ~

Priscilla

There was a young girl called Priscilla,
Who thought that she was a gorilla,
She went to a park,
And just for a lark,
She married an ape called Godzilla.

~ ~ ~ ~ ~

Poem That Deserved To Be Eaten

This poem was scrumptious,
This poem was tasty.
Now no-one will read it.
Why was I so hasty?

~ ~ ~ ~ ~

Professor John

Professor John put his trousers on
The top of his head one day.
Then, with a cough, he took them off
And threw them far away.
I asked him to say why he'd thrown them away,
And then to my surprise,
He blushed bright red before he said
That the flies got in his eyes.

~ ~ ~ ~ ~

Quizzical Poetical

1. Number the wives of Henry 8;
2. Battle of Hastings – give the date;
3. What would you put a helmet on?
4. What type of toy is Megatron?
5. Which planet's closest to the sun?
6. What animal was called Red Rum?
7. Which continent holds Timbuktu?
8. What's a bigger word for 'flu'?
9. What is the real name of Batman?
10. What would you say is a 'can-can'?
11. How many teeth are in your head?
12. What is the German word for 'bed'?
13. Who wrote *The Taming of the Shrew*?
14. Who invented the clerihew?
15. What would you find inside a hearse?
16. Was Florence Nightingale a nurse?
17. Which county is Southampton in?
18. Which painting has a great big grin?
19. What would do you if you rehearse?
20. Who is the writer of this verse?

And here's one I like the best:

21. Before they found Mount Everest,
Which mountain was higher than all the rest?

For answers you can take a look,
Find them at the end of this book,

~ ~ ~ ~ ~

Quintin's Scribble

Quintin is my brother,
He gurgles and he dribbles,
And when he talks it's very odd,
It's exactly like he scribbles,

Quintin's like no other,
He loves to munch and nibble,
But when he speaks, it's very strange,
It's as if he's speaking scribble.

Quintin's only twelve months,
He rarely has a quibble,
But when he does it's very cute,
When he tells us off in scribble.

~ ~ ~ ~ ~

Questions of Wasps

I never want to be a wasp,
Wasps are not for me
To sting and buzz? Make all that fuss?
I'd rather be a bee.

Bees make money with their honey,
Jars at fifty pee.
They build stout hives and live their lives
In quiet secrecy.

They always take good care of mum,
Giving her a comb.
They're good, sweet folk, who hate to smoke,
And take bright flowers home.

So when I see the bees at play,
I think of the wasp,
And ask a question that I'll mention:
What would you rather bee…

　　　　　…or a wasp?

~ ~ ~ ~ ~

Riddle

There are clues on every line to the eleven-letter answer

On the Isle of Lewis
They sing a Carroll
In the town of Borogove

They all snicker-snack
And drink their galumph
And dine out on Bander bird

They wock and jabber
They gimble and rath
And gyre to a slithy tove

While whiffling with sword
They tumtum the foe
And beamishly chortle joy

They frabjously play
Through the mimsy day
All frumious to the snatch

ANSWER: _ _ _ _ _ _ _ _ _ _ _

~ ~ ~ ~ ~

R.I.P. Stephen Morley

Old Stephen Morley
Woke up one day in bed
He thought that he was poorly
But he wasn't
He was dead

He looked so very peaceful
Lying there in death
But he never mentioned
He was only holding breath

+

**Here lies the body
Of poor old Stephen Morley
Who thought he was dead
When he was only poorly**

~ ~ ~ ~ ~

Reluctant Pig

Once, I owned a reluctant pig
I'd take it for a walk
I'd drag it all around the town
And try to sell pulled pork.

~ ~ ~ ~ ~

Smethurst and the Tom-Toms

Caruthers said to Smethurst,
"I say, do you hear those drums?"
"Don't bother me," said Smethurst,
"I'm busy with my sums."
"But Smethurst," said Caruthers,
"I think that you should answer,
It could be Charles, Caruthers,
Your friend the ballroom dancer."
"Don't pester me," said Smethurst
"I cannot stop to tarry,
To chat with any Tom-Tom,
Dick-Dick or Harry-Harry."

~ ~ ~ ~ ~

So Hungry I Could...

Once, when I was starving
And half-way through a horse,
I realised I wasn't
As hungry as I thought.

~ ~ ~ ~ ~

Spider

The spider owned eight spindly legs,
And loved them all like heaven,
When he looked down upon the ground,
There lay one, leaving seven.

The spider took another drink
Of beer with whisky mix,
Then he looked down and what he found
Meant his legs numbered six.

The spider scratched a puzzled brow,
Whilst breathing, 'Saints Alive',
And from his crown a leg dropped down,
Which meant he'd only five.

The spider looked a tortured look,
This was not entertaining,
And nearly died when he espied
He had but four remaining.

Poor spider span a silken web,
He was bereft of answers.
He tried to tie his legs to him,
But only found three dancers.

The spider took a longer drink,
Not knowing what to do,
And through his haze he dropped his gaze
On legs which numbered two.

Sad spider downed a larger drink,
To help him try to stop it,
But on the floor there was one more,
Poor spider had to hop it.

The spider watched his last leg fall,
By now he couldn't care less,
And as he drank, his eyelids sank,
This spider now was legless.

~ ~ ~ ~ ~

T

Once upon a time back in school,
My old teacher pointed at me,
And asked me to think of something
That began with the letter 'T'.
She wanted to know a subject
At which I was *not* very good,
But I just stared and looked at her
As if I had not understood.
Most of the kids started laughing,
Some of the others were yelling,
So, to shut them up I answered
"My worst thing of all - is 'Spelling'."

~ ~ ~ ~ ~

Tea is for Salad

Radishes, radishes,
I wonder where the radish is?
Can't wait to get my gnashers in,
When I find those radishes.

Lettuces, lettuces,
I wonder where the lettuce is?
Can't wait to take my lettuce in,
If the lettuce lets us in.

Cucumber, Cucumber,
All hail and praise the cucumber.
It's in the fridge that cucumber
It should be a cool-cumber.

Celery, celery,
Is he in the cellar he?
The downstairs room is cellar-y,
It's where I keep the celery.

Salad tea salad tea,
How I love a salad tea.
Radish, lettuce, cool-cumber,
And don't forget the celery!

~ ~ ~ ~ ~

Things I Have Seen

I've seen bat caves in Bolivia
And voles in Viet Nam
A starving horse in Hungary
Deep holes in Pakistan

I fought cats in Costa Rica
Ate bees in old Thailand
Watched sunsets in America
Sailed seas round Ireland

I've drunk tea inside a tee-pee,
In Belarus I danced
And then one day I watched some boys
Go tease a frog in France

I've seen things I cannot talk of
Events you'd not believe
Like grimalkins on fiery heaths
Things you could not conceive

Vampires in Transylvania
And mermaids in New York
Devils in dark Tasmania
Who giggle when they talk

A cockatrice in Latvia
A minotaur in Greece
Piranha fish in Liverpool
Who ate a scaly beast

I have seen the Niagara Falls
Completely freeze one night
And I have seen brave heroes
Fight darkness till it's light

But of all those many wonders
Of all those mystic scenes
There's one thing I have yet to see –
You - finishing your greens

~ ~ ~ ~ ~

Uncle

My uncle was killed when he swallowed his tuba,
It was a ghastly sight to see.
We buried him then on the south side of Cuba,
The funeral was very low key.

~ ~ ~ ~ ~

Universe is Chocolate

The universe is chocolate,
There's sweets among the stars,
Where you'll find treats so great to eat,
Like *Galaxy* and *Mars*.

You have *Revels* in a *Starburst*
And *Picnic* all the day,
When you take a *Flying Saucer*
Along the *Milky Way*.

~ ~ ~ ~ ~

Uranusquake

If there's an earthquake on Uranus,
What would it be called?
Would it be a *Uranusquake*?
I think we should be told.

~ ~ ~ ~ ~

Very Young Poet's Dilemma

The cat sat on the mat...?
What on earth is there that rhymes with that...?

~ ~ ~ ~ ~

Vegetarian's Search

Cabbages, cabbages,
I wonder where the cabbage is?
I've looked all round and in between,
Have you seen my delicious greens?

Potatoes, potatoes,
Where did they go, those potatoes?
I've now sent out potato spies,
I hope they use potato eyes.

Onions, onions,
I had some odd-shaped funny ones.
They disappeared, went out to hide,
You won't believe how much I've cried.

All my veg, all my veg,
I have lost my lovely veg.
I've only found a single bean:
A vegetarian has-been!

~ ~ ~ ~ ~

Very Weird Friends

I have friends that are weird, friends that are feared,
And there are those I think are rather cool.
There are some of them quite wise,
Others, nutters in disguise,
We're pretty much an ordinary school:

Frances goes to dances where she prances,
And Bunny likes to hop when at the bop.
Then Arthur makes advances
On anyone he fancies,
Until the dance is over then he'll stop.

Milly looks at Billy then is silly.
She'd like to take him back to her Grandma's,
They'd turn him in a jiffy
Straight into piccalilli
Then take him off to market in jam jars.

Grace is pulling faces at the races,
She's backed the horse she first saw on the course.
But it's not really funny
As she loses her money
And they have to take her off the course by force.

Jenny May Kilkenny stares at Benny
Who does the most outrageous belly flops.
So, then Jenny asks him why
He thinks he's a butterfly
And Benny says it's lovely when it stops.

Johnny says to Connie, "You look bonny",
He says it in the most convincing way.
It is then she takes command

Grabbing his fat, sweaty hand,
And now you see them wrestling every day.

Polly says, "Oh golly, I'm so jolly!
I'm such a happy person all the time."
But then she starts to hurry
Because there is a worry
That to be jolly must be thought a crime.

Denny has so many friends like Lenny.
Who's annoying and spoiling for a fight.
So when they go out for lunch
Lenny gets a rabbit punch,
Now Lenny knows that fighting isn't right.

Billy is a very silly Billy,
Sometimes you really don't know where to look.
There are days when he's a dog,
Then he's hopping like a frog,
Then lays an egg as if he is a duck.

Trevor cannot ever look at Heather,
It seems that he has fallen quite in love.
If she smiles at him a bit,
It's as if he has been hit
By a massive fist inside a boxing glove.

So, if all your friends drive you round the bend,
Remember it's the same inside a zoo.
From the weird ones to the meek,
Every creature is unique,
We're all just human beings through and through.

~ ~ ~ ~ ~

William Shakespeare

William Shakespeare
Would sometimes appear
As an actor upon the Globe stage,
But his acting was not all the rage.

~ ~ ~ ~ ~

Winner of the Naughty Limerick Competition

Tee-tumpity tumpity tum
Tee-tumpity tumpity tum
Tee-tumpity tee
Tee-tumpity tee
Tee-tumpity tumpity bum

Young poets are welcome to create their own naughty limerick which they think will be better than this winner of the competition.

~ ~ ~ ~ ~

Why I Hate Sourdough Toast

They say that sourdough's good for you,
They say the whole world knows,
But when you melt the butter on,
It drips through on your toes.

They tell me sourdough's healthy,
As good as crisp fresh greens,
But when you melt the butter on,
It drips down on your jeans.

They tell me sourdough's trendy,
So chic and such a treat,
But when you melt the butter on,
It drips upon your feet.

They brag that sourdough's different,
And goes so well with eggs,
But when you melt the butter on,
It drips along your legs.

They say sourdough's traditional,
Though you must be alert,
But when you melt the butter on,
It drips through on your shirt.

Sourdough bread's the best there is,
So everyone agrees,
But when you melt the butter on,
It ends up on your knees.

So if you don't want butter,
Spoiling all your clothes,
Eat rye bread, wheatgerm anything
But sourdough toasted loaves.

~ ~ ~ ~ ~

Xmas

Please don't think me a failure,
An ass or a fool or a peasant,
But Xmas past is not for me,
I prefer a Xmas present.

~ ~ ~ ~ ~

Xara's Bomb

I'm going to make a Bomb,
That's what I'll call the dress
I will design,
In record time,
In order to impress.

And when I put it on,
The bomb and I will BOOM!
We'll stun the Prom
When me and Bomb
Explode into that room!

~ ~ ~ ~ ~

X's = Kisses

Around about one Xmas-time,
An X came out to walk.
Upon his way he met a friend,
And they began to talk.

"What brings you here?" the first X said,
"Could it be for the fun?
Or have you come to stroll around
Beneath the setting sun?"

The second X said, "Not at all,
It's you I've come to seek,
For do you know that we've not met
For longer than a week?

Why is it you've forsaken me?
You know I love you so,
Why did you ever move away,
Why ever did you go?"

The first X looked around about,
And blushing looked away
Towards the shining meadow grass,
And thought just what to say.

"I love you too," he said at last,
"I'll love you ever more,
But I could never marry you,
For I'll be ever poor."

The second X said, "Worry not,
It's you that I have missed,
Not gold or wealth or riches..."
                    ...and so the X's XXXXed.

~ ~ ~ ~ ~

Y?

Of all the alphabet letters
I'm friends with twenty-five.
"Why only twenty-five?" you ask,
I'm afraid I don't know why.

~ ~ ~ ~ ~

Yawn

The yawn is a terrible sneak-up thing,
It creeps up without warning,
Just when the school bell starts to ring,
You suddenly find you're yawning.

The yawn is a horrible crafty wain,
Don't ever ask for warning,
For when the teacher calls your name,
You answer, 'Here,' while yawning.

The Yawn isn't sensible nor admired,
For leaving out its warning,
'Cos when you're asked if you are tired
You just can't stop your yawning.

The Yawn means trouble for everyone,
One and all without warning,
For though we've slept twelve hours plus one,
We never can stop yawning.

~ ~ ~ ~ ~

Yodelling

If   I   yodel,
  only could

How   I   be,
  happy would

  I'd the
   be best,

 Beat the
  all   rest

Of yodelling -tern- -ty!
 the fra- -i-

~ ~ ~ ~ ~

Zoomorphic Me

I really am zoomorphic,
I change without a care.
One minute I'm the same old me,
The next, I am a bear.

And if the mood should take me,
Standing in a station,
Instead of getting on the train –
I'm in hibernation.

And when at last I wake up,
And feel I need to jog,
I simply change myself again
Into a greyhound dog.

It's fun being zoomorphic.
When I've just had a bath,
I'll look into the mirror and
A hippo makes me laugh.

Zoomorphic me is happy,
I change myself to suit,
If I can't reach the trees then a
Giraffe will pick the fruit.

If I should meet a person
Who bores me fit to snore,
I simply turn into a pig,
And show him who's a boar.

And should I find a bully,
Who sneers with every breath,
Into a tiger I will turn
And scare him half to death.

Of course, I am endangered,
The last one of my kind,
But lots of us are changeable,
It's just a state of mind.

~ ~ ~ ~ ~

Zig-Zag

Zig-zag, zig-zag, oh zig-zag,
Why do you never see,
It is so much easier
To go from **A** to **B**?

Why do you ever need to
Go via letter **C**,
Then stop off at **D**, **E**, **F**,
Or visit letter **G**?

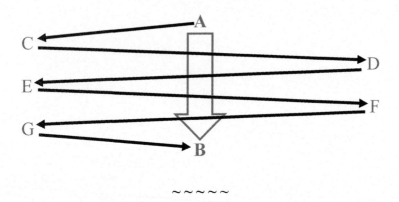

~ ~ ~ ~ ~

Zed to Ay

Zed is always left aside, right to the very end,
Wy is never far behind – Wy is Zed's only friend.
Ekks is very, very nice, signed with a loving kiss,
Double Yoo is put down twice, in case the first you miss.
Vee comes after single Yoo, before the Double, too,
Yoo is all alone you know and sobs the whole night through.
Tee is happy all the day and laughs Tee-hee, tee-hee,
Ess does not know what to say but knows what she can see.
Arr is gasping out with pain, it's hot under his feet,
Kyew is hiding from the rain, his tail beneath his seat.
Pee is hopping up and down, bursting with the strain,
Ohh looks on and bears a frown, he really is quite vain.
Enn is very dignified, there's nothing he derides,
Emm is ever mystified, but she can see both sides.
Ell is nearly always hot, from lying underground,
Kay just loves to trot and trot, then jump in one long bound.
Jay is very insular, making her real snotty,
Aye sees all there is to see, which makes her rather dotty.
Aitch just loves to sing and sing, the others block their ears
Gee cannot believe a thing he sees or smells or hears,
Eff is rather frightening, she screams and swears and sneers,
Eee is like greased lightning and runs away in tears.
Dee has put on too much weight, which makes him stretch his
back,
See is never ever late, in case she gets the sack.
Bee has got a double chin, which he thinks is a crime,
But Ay just loves to start it all, that's why she hates this
rhyme.

~ ~ ~ ~ ~

THE END   *…or is it…?*

PS...

MOSQUITO

by Max Morley when aged 9

The mosquito is a horrible creature,
Sucking blood is its main feature.
If there's a lump where your skin is pink,
That means the mosquito has had a drink.

The mosquito is a horrible creature,
Sucking blood is its main feature
At night it will come out to meet ya,
Put on some spray or it'll eat ya!

~~~~~

Quizzical Poetical Answers

1. Six
2. 1066
3. Your head
4. A Transformer
5. Mercury
6. A (race) horse
7. Africa
8. Influenza
9. Bruce Wayne
10. A dance
11. 32
12. Bett
13. William Shakespeare
14. Edmund Clerihew Bentley
15. A coffin
16. Yes
17. Hampshire
18. *The Laughing Cavalier*
19. Prepare something
20. See the front cover
21. Mount Everest (of course!)

Also Available from Amazon

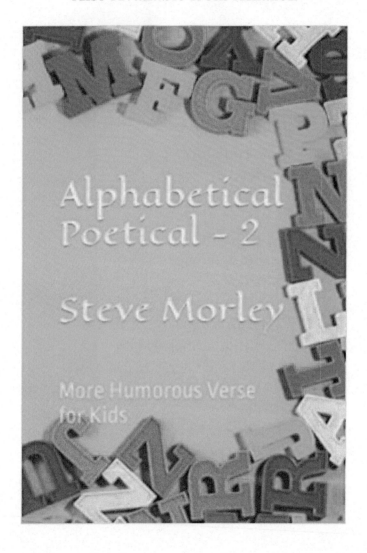

Also Available from Amazon

Alphabetical
Poetical - 3

Steve Morley

Yet More Humorous Verse For Kids

Also Available from Amazon

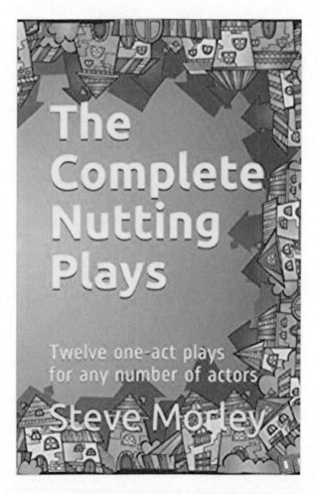

Nutting is a town where everybody lives ordinary lives in an extraordinary way, and where everyone who lives there is known as a Nutter.

Printed in Great Britain
by Amazon